MUSEUM
MYSTERIES

Museum Mysteries is published by Stone Arch Books
A Capstone Imprint
1710 Roe Crest Drive
North Mankato, MN 56003
www.mycapstonepub.com

Library of Congress Cataloging-in-Publication Data is available on the Library of
Congress website.

ISBN 978-1-4965-2519-2 (hardcover) — ISBN 978-1-4965-2523-9 (paperback) —
ISBN 978-1-4965-2527-7 (eBook PDF) — ISBN (978-1-4965-3331-9) (reflowable epub)

Summary: A ghost has been spotted lurking around Capitol City's American History
Museum. Can Raining Sam and his friends figure out who's behind the haunting before
someone gets hurt?

Designer: K. Carlson
Editor: A. Deering
Production Specialist: K. McColley

Photo Credits: Shutterstock (vector images, backgrounds, paper textures)

Printed and bound in Canada.
009637F16

The Case of the
SOLDIER'S GHOST

By Steve Brezenoff
Illustrated by Lisa K. Weber

STONE ARCH BOOKS
a capstone imprint

The Vietnam War

- The Vietnam War occurred in Vietnam, Laos, and Cambodia from November 1955 until the fall of Saigon in April 1975.

- The Vietnam War is the longest war in which the United States has participated.

- Prior to the war, Vietnam, a small country in Southeast Asia, was separated into North Vietnam and South Vietnam. North Vietnam was communist and wanted to end U.S. support to South Vietnam and combine the two halves into one country.

- The Vietnam War was extremely unpopular back in the United States. Many people participated in demonstations protesting the war.

- Nearly sixty thousand U.S. soldiers were killed in the war. More than one hundred and fifty thousand were injured, and more than two thousand four hundred soldiers are still missing.

Amal Farah

Raining Sam

Wilson Kipper

Clementine Wim

Capitol City Sleuths

Amal Farah
Age: 11
Favorite Museum: Air and Space Museum
Interests: astronomy, space travel, and
building models of spaceships

Raining Sam
Age: 12
Favorite Museum: American History Museum
Interests: Ojibwe history, culture, and
traditions, American history — good and bad

Clementine Wim
Age: 13
Favorite Museum: Art Museum
Interests: painting, sculpting with clay, and
anything colorful

Wilson Kipper
Age: 10
Favorite Museum: Natural History Museum
Interests: dinosaurs (especially pterosaurs
and herbivores) and building dinosaur models

TABLE OF

CONTENTS

CHAPTER 1
A Dark, Stormy Night

It was after closing time when Raining Sam and his friend Amal Farah wandered the darkened halls of the Capitol City American History Museum. The museum might be closed to the public, but the two kids were allowed to wander — as long as they didn't touch anything — because Raining's father worked at the museum.

"Are you going to the Fourth of July party?" Amal said as they walked along the main corridor. The galleries on either side were almost completely dark, lit only by the glowing red exit signs that dotted the walls and ceilings. Outside, a summer thunderstorm was kicking into high gear.

"I think so," Raining said. He shoved his hands into his pockets. "If my dad doesn't have to work, that is."

"It's a national holiday!" Amal said. "The museum will be closed."

"The museum is closed now!" Raining pointed out. But his dad was working that very moment, which is why Raining and Amal were wandering the halls, waiting for him to finish up for the day.

"Okay, good point," Amal admitted. "But still. The museums are throwing the party. He'll probably go, right?" She knew all about the event since her father worked at the Air and Space Museum. The duo's other best friends — Clementine Wim and Winston Kipper — each also had a parent who worked at a Capitol City museum. It was how they'd all become such good friends.

"Probably," Raining said as they reached the huge archway at the end of the corridor. Beyond that were the shadowy figures inside the gallery, lit dimly under the exit signs.

Suddenly lightning cracked, lighting up the big gallery and its archway for an instant. A moment later, thunder boomed and shook the world.

Raining turned around. "Let's go back."

But Amal kept walking. "What's in there?" she said. "Isn't that the gallery that's always been closed?"

Raining stopped. "Under construction," he corrected. "They finished last week. It's the new Vietnam War exhibit."

Amal nodded and walked slowly on. "I want to see it," she said.

"It's too *dark* to see," Raining said.

"My eyes will adjust," Amal insisted. "But you can wait out here if you're too scared." With that, she stepped through the archway and vanished into the darkness.

Raining sighed and rolled his eyes. He'd already seen the exhibit — he'd been there when it opened. But he didn't love the idea of standing in front of that giant, dark archway just waiting for Amal to pop back out. So he stepped inside too.

"Amal!" Raining called into the darkness as he moved slowly through the gallery. He'd been inside once, but he didn't know by heart where everything was, and he sure didn't want to start bumping into things. "Where are you?"

"Oof!" Amal grunted in response. Obviously she *had* bumped into something.

"You okay?" Raining asked, doing his best to follow Amal's voice through the darkness. Lightning cracked again, and for an instant, the gallery was illuminated. Raining thought he saw Amal to his left, hunched over, and started in that direction.

"I'm fine," Amal called back. Strangely, her voice seemed to come from behind him now. "But you were right. I can't see a thing in here except when there's some lightning."

"Let's go then," Raining said, turning around. "Head for the doorway."

"Just a sec," Amal replied. This time her voice seemed to come from clear across the gallery, near the huge windows overlooking the Big Lawn that connected all the museums in the Capitol City collection. "I can see a little if I stand over by the window."

Raining rolled his eyes and walked with his hands in front of him, feeling his way around the diorama in the center of the gallery. Finally, as another bolt of lightning streaked across the sky, he saw Amal's silhouette against the huge window.

"What are you looking at?" Raining asked as he approached.

"I'm not sure." Amal stood before a trio of life-size soldiers — mannequins, really — and squinted at the plaque in front of them. "I can't read in this light."

"We'll come back tomorrow," Raining said. "Let's go. Dad will be done soon."

"Fine, fine," Amal said.

Raining led her back through the gallery, around the diorama in the middle, and toward the big archway. As they reached it, lightning struck again.

Raining and Amal both turned and looked back into the gallery at the same time. In the brief instant it was illuminated by the lightning bolt, a hunched-over figure hurried across the rear of the gallery. He was carrying something in his hands.

"Did you see that?" Raining asked.

Amal nodded. "A soldier."

"He had a helmet on," Raining said.

"It must have been a trick of the light. From the lightning strike," Amal whispered.

"There was no one else in the gallery a second ago, right?" Raining asked as Amal looped her arm into his elbow.

"Right," Amal said. "So it must have been a trick of the light."

Together they backed away from the huge archway.

"Because if it wasn't . . . ," Raining said.

"Then it was a ghost," Amal finished.

Lightning and thunder struck together just then, lighting up the gallery and shaking the museum. Raining and Amal screamed, turned around, and ran back to Dr. Sam's office.

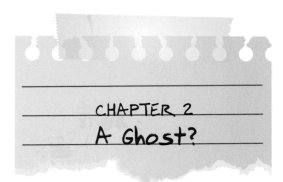

CHAPTER 2
A Ghost?

"Wow," Clementine Wim said later that night. Her face filled one of the two rectangular boxes on the screen of Raining's laptop. Wilson Kipper's face filled its own rectangular box next to hers. "You saw a ghost!"

Wilson rolled his eyes. "What happened next?" he asked through the computer. "Did you go back in to investigate?"

"No," Raining said, leaning toward the screen. "We played cards on the floor of my dad's office until he was ready to leave."

"Why didn't you go check it out?" Wilson said.

"Oh, please," Amal said. She was pacing back and forth across the floor in Raining's bedroom. "Don't pretend like you wouldn't have been scared."

"Of course I wouldn't have," Wilson said. "There's no such thing as ghosts."

Clementine smiled and shook her head. "Oh, Wilson," she said. "I adore you, but you're *so* naïve."

"I don't think it was a ghost either," Raining said. "I think it was just a trick of the light. Lightning struck, and there are all those mannequins of soldiers in that gallery. It just *looked* like one of them moved."

"Maybe," Amal said, leaning down next to Raining to look into the laptop's camera. "But it sure looked like a person to me."

"Then maybe it *was* a person," Wilson said. "It's not like there's a shortage of people in any of the museums. But that doesn't mean it was a ghost. It was probably an employee."

"Then where did he go?" Raining asked.

On the screen, Wilson shrugged. "Through a door?" he suggested.

"Maybe we should investigate," Amal said. "Even if it wasn't a ghost, it was . . . I don't know . . . weird."

"Of course we should investigate!" Clementine exclaimed. "I already have so many books and articles on ghost sightings. Museums are often the location of tremendous spiritual activity, you know."

"This is ridiculous," Wilson said.

"Oh, shush," Clementine said. Despite their three-year age difference, she and Wilson were best friends. They knew just how to push each other's buttons.

"Fine," Wilson said, rolling his eyes. "Let's meet tomorrow morning at the American History Museum. See you then."

* * *

The next morning, Amal, Clementine, and Wilson met at the American History Museum as soon as it opened. Raining was already there waiting for them; his dad had gone in early to catch up on work, so Raining had joined him.

When his friends arrived, Raining led them straight to the new Vietnam War gallery and pointed out the soldiers near the back window. "I think the lightning must have cast a funny shadow on the three soldiers near the window," he said. "The way the light flickered could have made it look like they were moving."

"I think you're right," Wilson said. He ran ahead and stopped at the window, then turned to face the mannequins. Clementine hurried after him.

"You know," Amal said, stepping up next to Raining, "this place isn't nearly as creepy in daylight."

Raining nodded. With visitors solemnly strolling through the gallery, and with the photos lining the walls — some black and white, some color, but all very dreary — the whole thing seemed a bit melancholy.

"Hey, Raining!" Wilson called from across the gallery, shattering the quiet.

A few of the other visitors turned to glare at him. A few even shushed him.

"Sorry," Wilson added meekly.

Raining hurried across the gallery with Amal at his side. "What are you shouting about?" he asked.

"I didn't know anyone would care," Wilson said. "People shout at my mom's museum all the time." Dr. Carolyn Kipper worked at the nearby Museum of Natural History.

Clementine closed her eyes and shook her head gravely. "Never," she said. "At the Capitol City Art Museum, our visitors have the utmost respect for silent contemplation."

Raining shook his head at Clementine's silliness. "Wilson, what are you shouting about?" he asked again.

Wilson pointed at the soldiers near the window. "You said there were three."

"Right," Raining said, nodding. "Three soldiers — wait a minute."

Amal grabbed his hand as a chill ran up his back. "There *were* three here last night," she said. "Now there are two."

"They took one out?" Clementine said.

Raining shook his head. "Last night," he said, "one of them wasn't a mannequin."

CHAPTER 3
Time to Investigate

"I can't believe it," Amal said later that morning. The four friends were sitting together in the museum cafeteria having a midmorning snack of granola bars, juice, and fruit. "We were standing inches away from a real *ghost*."

Raining couldn't believe it either. He didn't know *what* to believe. But when he'd realized that one of the soldiers he and Amal had stood next to during the thunderstorm hadn't been a mannequin, he'd almost fainted. He'd had to sit down before he passed out.

"It wasn't a ghost," Wilson said.

"Then what was it?" Amal said.

"A person," Wilson said. "A very creepy person, but a person nonetheless."

"Wearing a uniform in the museum after hours?" Amal said. She shook her head. "It doesn't make sense."

"And where did he go?" Raining said. That was the one thing that really bothered him. Logically, he didn't think the figure they'd seen could have been a ghost, but whoever it was had vanished as suddenly as he'd appeared. And there was only one way out of that gallery.

"We looked into that, actually," Clementine said, sitting up. "I mean, while you were resting."

Raining felt his face go hot. He'd almost fainted once before — when he'd cut his thumb while trying to help his mom slice onions — but never in front of his friends.

"Anyway, while you were sitting on the floor with your eyes closed," Wilson continued, "I did some looking around."

"Looking for what?" Raining asked, taking a bite of his banana. Amal had made him get it. She'd insisted it would be good, quick energy after his near-fainting spell in the gallery.

"Doors," Wilson said. "There are three of them, besides the big archway into the main corridor."

"There are?" Raining said. "I didn't think there were any other ways out."

"Two of them are hidden," Wilson explained. "They're plain white doors on a plain white wall, and there are pieces of the exhibit set conveniently in front of them, so visitors won't notice."

"What about the third one?" Amal asked him.

"That's the emergency exit," Wilson replied. "I obviously didn't open it, since an alarm would probably go off. It probably leads to a staircase down to the Big Lawn. We can check it out from the outside later."

"But what about the hidden doors?" Raining asked. He was beginning to feel a little better now.

"I figured they were storage," Wilson said. "One of them was locked, so that's probably what it was, but the other one swung open."

"And?" Amal said, leaning forward in her seat.

"An office," Wilson said, sounding dejected. "Or a workshop. Something like that. A bunch of grown-ups in white coats were sitting around a table with papers and computers and tablets and stuff."

"Oops," Raining said. "Did you get in trouble?"

"Nope," Clementine said. "I stuck my head in and said, 'Did you guys see a ghost come through here last night?'"

Wilson dropped his head onto the tabletop and groaned.

"They said they hadn't," Clementine finished. "But they all looked at me like I was crazy."

"Imagine that," Wilson said, his voice muffled by the table.

Just then, Raining's father hurried into the cafeteria. "There you are!" he said when he spotted Raining and his friends at their table. He walked quickly over to them, slammed his hands on their table, and said, "Do you know what kind of madness you've caused in this museum?"

The friends blinked at one another. Raining looked up at his father. "We did?" he said. "How?"

"Half the staff of the museum is in a panic!" Mr. Sam said.

"Why?" Wilson asked.

"Because you four," Mr. Sam said, casting his angriest glare over the four friends, one by one, "have somehow managed to start a rumor that a *ghost* is haunting the museum!"

CHAPTER 4
Growing Panic

Later that evening, the four friends stood in the main lobby where it met up with the museum's central corridor. The museum would be closing soon, but the lobby was crowded — more crowded than Raining had ever seen it. By now the ghost story had spread not only among the staff, but among the visitors, as well, and no one seemed interested in leaving.

"How did this happen?" Raining asked, looking around at the crowds still milling about.

"We didn't tell anyone about what happened," Amal said. "Not even Raining's dad."

Wilson, Raining, and Amal turned and looked at Clementine. "What?" she said. "Why are you all looking at me?"

"Because *you* told a roomful of museum staff about a ghost this morning, remember?" Wilson said.

"Oh, that?" Clementine said. "You think they took me seriously?"

"Even if only one of them did," Raining said, "that could be enough to start people talking."

"Well, people are talking all right," Amal said, looking around at the crowd in the lobby.

Sure enough, everyone whispered and chattered and shouted and squealed about ghosts — scary ghosts and friendly ghosts, romantic ghosts and tragic ghosts, the ghosts of soldiers and the ghosts of queens.

Just then, the public address speakers overhead crackled. "Museum visitors," boomed the voice of the lead security officer, "the museum is now closing. Please make your way to the main exit on the east side of the museum at this time. Thank you."

A few people looked disappointed, but the majority of the crowd quieted and began moving toward the doors.

"Let's stick around after closing," Wilson said. "Maybe we can have a look around and see if our ghost impostor left any clues."

"If it *was* an impostor," Clementine said.

"I'll check with my dad," Raining said. "He's probably working late again."

"I most certainly am not," Mr. Sam said, appearing behind his son. He grabbed Raining's shoulder and steered him firmly toward the door. "Let's go home. Now."

Raining frowned at his friends. "Sorry, guys," he said, letting his dad pull him toward the exit. "Looks like no more snooping around tonight!"

* * *

After supper at home, Raining lay on his bed and stared at the little window opposite him. It was pouring, and he liked to watch the drops run down the glass, lit by the light from the streetlamp at the corner. Just then, his computer chirped, signaling an incoming call.

Raining hopped up and hurried to his desk. He clicked on "answer" and Clementine's face filled the screen.

"So," Clementine started, not even saying hello. Her eyes moved quickly, up and down, like she was reading something onscreen while she talked. "I've been researching the Vietnam War, and I mean, we learned a tiny bit about it last year, but I didn't know a *lot* of this stuff."

"Like what?" Raining asked. He was a year behind Clementine in school, but American history was one of his hobbies. He knew quite a bit about the Vietnam War.

"Well, for starters," Clementine continued, "it was a very *unpopular* war."

"I know," Raining said. He'd read and seen movies about the protests during the war. People would march in the streets, carrying signs decrying the war.

"And a lot of the soldiers didn't even want to be in the Army," Clementine went on. "They got *drafted*."

"I know that too," Raining said. The draft had dictated that any man older than eighteen might be forced to go to war or else to jail. Some teenagers had tried to hide from the draft. Some had even run off to Canada or Europe so they wouldn't have to fight.

"And then when the people who fought got home," Clementine continued, leaning closer to the webcam, "some of them were still seriously injured. And they weren't treated very well."

Raining knew that too. His grandfather had been in the Vietnam War. When he'd returned home, he'd spent years in a wheelchair. After lots of physical therapy, he'd been able to walk, but always with a cane and never very well.

"Clementine," Raining said, cutting her off before she could tell him more, "why are you telling me this stuff?"

"Don't you see?" Clementine said, looking right into the camera. Her eyes went wide and solemn. "Ghosts always have a reason to *haunt*."

"A reason?" Raining repeated.

"Of course!" Clementine exclaimed. She jumped up from her seat and disappeared from view. Raining could still hear her calling from across her family's library — that's what they called the little room with the computer and a big collection of art books. She returned carrying a book that looked older than Capitol City. It was bound in red leather, cracked at the edges, and had a gold ribbon dangling from its pages.

Clementine opened the book to where the ribbon was. "Ghosts," she read, "and other *malevolent* spirits have been offended in life. They linger among the living, tormenting them, until the wrongs have been righted." She clapped the book closed and bit her lip.

"So?" Raining said.

"So," Clementine said, "the wrong that must be righted is the Vietnam War — the terrible way this poor soldier was probably treated in life!"

Raining sighed heavily. He liked Clementine — she was one of his best friends — but sometimes she just seemed so . . . *out there.*

"What are we supposed to do about it?" he said. "It's not like we can go back in time and stop the war! Besides, like a million protestors *tried* to stop the war, and they couldn't. It went on for years!"

Clementine narrowed her eyes and grinned. "I have some ideas," she said. "I'll see you tomorrow, okay? Bye!"

"Um," Raining said as the box with Clementine's freckled face flickered to black and closed, "bye."

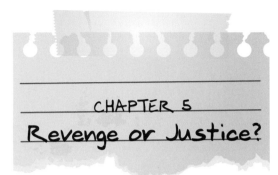

CHAPTER 5
Revenge or Justice?

The next morning, Raining pulled on a T-shirt and dragged himself downstairs. Dad sat in the living room on the edge of the couch. He hadn't shaved, and his hair was a mess. He looked positively exasperated as he stared at the morning news on the TV.

"What's wrong?" Raining asked.

Dad jumped and looked over his shoulder. "Oh, Raining," he said, forcing

a little smile. "It's you. Nothing, nothing."
He clicked off the TV and stood up. "You
coming down to the museum with me this
morning?"

"Sure," Raining said.

"Great," Dad said. He patted Raining's
shoulder. "We'll leave in five minutes."

"Okay," Raining said.

When Dad was out of earshot, Raining
clicked the TV on again. The local news
anchor talked about the upcoming Fourth
of July festival at the Big Lawn. No reason
that would upset Dad so much.

Raining hit the rewind button on the
DVR remote and zipped past stories about
baseball games, some big renovation
downtown, and the American History
Museum.

"Whoa," Raining said, hitting play. "What's this?"

Onscreen, the anchorwoman smiled as she said, "The exhibits at the Capitol City American History Museum are no longer happy just standing still. According to several local sources, including one young woman close to the museum's upper management, the American soldiers in the Vietnam War gallery" — she paused for effect — "have come to life."

The picture switched to a young woman's face, which had been blurred out so the viewer couldn't identify her. But Raining would have known who it was with no picture at all. He knew her voice well enough — Clementine Wim.

"They haven't come to life exactly," the blurred-out version of Clementine said.

"Rather, one American soldier is haunting the exhibit — like a poltergeist. He wants us to know he's angry."

"What is he angry about?" a reporter asked offscreen.

"Vietnam veterans were treated terribly," Clementine said. "Many of them didn't want to join the Army in the first place."

"So the ghosts are back for revenge?" the reporter asked.

Clementine shook her head. "Not revenge," she said. "I don't think they'll hurt anyone. They just want justice."

The picture switched back to the newsroom. "Justice," the anchorwoman said, her face stern and serious now. "But how can we, the people of Capitol City, hope to undo the injustices of decades past?" She laughed lightly. "I don't know, but if you want a chance at seeing the poltergeists, the museum is open from nine to six all weekend, but closed on Monday for July Fourth."

Raining clicked off the TV. Behind him, someone coughed, and Raining turned around. Dad was standing there.

"Are you mad?" Raining said. He hated to think his father would be mad at him and his friends.

Dad shook his head. "No, I'm not mad. But the museum is likely to be mobbed today, and this is all going to take some untangling. So I'll be working late tonight." He grabbed his keys from the coffee table and said, "Let's go."

CHAPTER 6
A Madhouse

Just like Raining's dad said, the museum was a madhouse that day. Raining and his friends could barely get *into* the Vietnam War gallery, let alone look around for clues. They finally gave up and spent most of the day roaming the other exhibits or lying around on the Big Lawn, watching as the Fourth of July festivities were set up.

As the afternoon cooled into early evening, the museum crowds began to thin.

Raining and his friends hung out on the couches in the staff lounge near Dr. Sam's office until after six o'clock, when the museum officially closed.

With the staff busy trying to solve the "poltergeist problem," the kids had free reign of the museum. Raining led them out of the staff-only area, toward the Vietnam War gallery.

"Finally," Wilson said, "we can find out just what is going on here."

"I *think* we already know," Clementine said. She winked at Raining.

Raining grunted in irritation.

"What?" Clementine said, seeming surprised by his reaction.

"I can't believe you went on the news and told the whole world there are *ghosts* at the museum!" Raining said, shaking his head. He'd kept his mouth shut about it all day, but he couldn't take it anymore.

"You were on the news?" Amal said, her eyes wide. She smiled and nodded. "Cool."

Wilson sighed. "Is that why the place was so crazy today?" he said.

Clementine crossed her arms and lifted her chin. "I will do what I think is right until justice has been served for the poltergeist haunting this gallery," she said, sounding even more mature than usual.

They had reached the Vietnam War gallery. Outside, the sun was low, and the room was lit up in a fiery sunset orange.

"There they are," Amal said, nodding toward the soldiers by the window. "Just two of them."

"Did you think the third one — the ghost — would be standing there waiting for us?" Wilson said with a laugh.

"No," Amal said.

"I was hoping he'd be here," Clementine said. "If we're going to help him, we might have to try to communicate with him."

"You're even kookier than usual," Wilson said. He strode across the gallery toward the soldier mannequins.

Clementine stomped her foot. "You two," she said, snarling at the boys.

"What did we do?" Raining asked.

"You don't believe me!" Clementine snapped. She grabbed Amal's hand and pulled her toward the gallery exit. "Come on. We'll find the ghost *on our own*."

As Amal got dragged away, she looked back over her shoulder at Raining and shrugged, giving him a "What am I supposed to do?" look.

"Where are they going?" Wilson asked as he came back from the mannequins.

"I think Clementine is mad at you," Raining said. "And possibly at me."

Wilson shrugged. "She'll get over it," he said. "Besides, I'm a man of science. I'm not going to pretend ghosts are real just to spare her feelings."

"She's your best friend!" Raining said.

Wilson stared at Raining for a moment, as if waiting for him to say something else. When Raining didn't say anything else, Wilson said, "We should split up and look around."

"In here?" Raining said. It wasn't a very big gallery.

Wilson shook his head. "The whole museum," he said. "We have no idea what we're looking for, but we do know that your *ghost* appeared after hours. This is a good time to really investigate."

Raining didn't think there was anything to investigate. What he'd seen the other night had been a trick of the light and his frayed nerves during the thunderstorm. But the truth was, he could use some time to wander the museum on his own. His friends were all getting on his nerves today.

"All right," Raining said. "I'll go check the south wing."

Wilson nodded, pulled out a flashlight, and left the gallery.

"I guess you'll take the north wing,"
Raining said to the empty gallery. Then he
sighed and strolled off toward the Colonial
exhibit.

CHAPTER 7
Footsteps

Wilson ducked in and out of the galleries in the north wing, moving quickly. He didn't expect to find anything, so there was no need to linger. Before too long, he'd checked every gallery in the wing and had seen nothing of interest to the case — if this even *was* a case.

When he was finished with his investigation, Wilson ended up in the big front entrance. It looked especially eerie after hours. The gate was down in front of the glass doors, so the silvery light from the streetlamps out front fell across the floor in a series of long, skinny lines.

Wilson sat down on one of the long wooden benches in the center of the lobby. The benches formed a square around the central statue of Lady Liberty — not a copy of the massive statue in New York Harbor but one inspired by it. Her torch was held high above her under the domed skylight. It almost looked like they'd put the skylight there just so the statue could raise her torch.

Footsteps approached, but given the way they echoed around the big lobby,

Wilson couldn't tell which wing they were coming from. They seemed to be coming from every direction at once.

Wilson stood up and pulled his super-bright mini flashlight back out of his pocket. First he shined it down the south wing, where he'd just come from — nothing. Next he shined it up the north wing — nothing there either.

Turning in a circle, Wilson shined it up the central corridor, toward the Vietnam War gallery, and something moved. It looked like a figure, halfway up the corridor, but it was gone as quickly as it had appeared.

Wilson moved slowly along the main corridor, his flashlight beam shining in front of him, lighting the way. It helped a little, but it was a narrow beam and couldn't light the entire hallway at once. The footsteps were up ahead, though. Wilson was sure of it. And they were moving away from him, toward the Vietnam War gallery.

"I'm not scared," Wilson whispered to himself. Then he called out loud, "Who's up there?"

No one replied, but the footsteps stopped, so Wilson stopped too.

"Is that you, Raining?" he called out, hoping his friend would answer.

No reply. Wilson shined his light back and forth, up and down the corridor. It was empty.

Ahead on the right were two elevator doors. Opposite them sat the men's and women's bathrooms, a water fountain, and a custodian's closet.

But no people.

Wilson took a deep breath and walked on, shining the light as he went. He held his breath as he passed the bathroom doors, but on a hunch he tried the men's room — it was locked. All the doors were locked, and the elevators were turned off for the night.

He was alone.

But the footsteps . . . , Wilson thought.

In spite of being a man of science — one who didn't believe in ghosts — Wilson was scared. With the flashlight beam bouncing around the corridor in front of him, he took off running, not stopping until he reached the Vietnam War gallery.

And there, as he hurried through the big archway, Wilson knocked right into someone. The flashlight flew from his hand, hit the floor, and switched off, casting the entire room in darkness.

CHAPTER 8
A Real Haunting?

Clementine and Amal, meanwhile, had separated as well — but quite by accident.

Her disagreement with Wilson had left Clementine in despair, and her first stop was the staff restroom, the only one unlocked after hours. "I just want to splash my face," she said as she pushed open the door. "I'll be right out."

"I'm going to look around," Amal said.

"Don't go far!" Clementine called through the closing door. She turned to the mirror and added quietly, "I don't want to be alone in this haunted museum."

Clementine studied her reflection. Her hair was a mess. Her cheeks were splotchy red. She splashed cold water on her face and wrestled her hair into a bun. "Am I being silly?" she asked. "Is it crazy to think there really *is* a ghost in the history museum?

Unfortunately the reflection had no reply.

Clementine took a deep breath. "No," she told herself. The reflection looked sure, even if that's not how Clementine was feeling on the inside. "It's not crazy, and you're not silly. Veterans haven't been treated well. Even if I'm wrong about everything else, I'm not wrong about wanting to help."

With that, Clementine nodded, turned away from the mirror, and pushed open the door. The hallway was empty.

"Amal?" Clementine called up the corridor. Her voice echoed back to her, giving her a chill. "Amal, I said don't go far!"

No one replied. Amal didn't appear from around a corner. Clementine was alone.

"I'll find Dr. Sam," Clementine told herself, setting her shoulders. "His office is back here somewhere, right?" She'd been there a dozen times or more. But without Raining to guide her, she wasn't sure she could find it again. Still, there was no sense standing there feeling scared and lost.

So Clementine walked deeper into the staff-only section of the museum, past closed doors and open doors, all the offices beyond long since dark. In the near silence, she heard every creak and breath of the museum itself, as if the building were a restless beast.

Clementine had an active imagination. What she did not have, however, was a very good sense of direction. Before she knew it, Clementine had left the staff-only area and wandered into the huge Hall of Presidents.

In the dark, the gallery was hardly recognizable. And though a quiet and confident part of Clementine's brain knew that the 43 figures looming over her were merely mannequins of the 43 United States presidents, the louder part of her brain — the imaginative and frightened part — saw something else entirely.

Screaming, Clementine turned and fled from the gallery. She didn't make it far, though. Almost immediately she found herself face to face with the double doors that lead to the museum's auditorium — doors that were locked this late at night.

Clementine turned and pressed her back to the locked doors. She faced the looming mannequins and tried to slow her panicked breath.

"Okay, Clementine," she said to herself. "You're *fine*. Don't freak out. They're just statues. They can't hurt you."

Despite the brave words, Clementine wasn't feeling very brave. The gallery's main exit was clear across the room. In the darkness, she couldn't make out the presidents' friendly smiles or sparkling lapel pins or familiar chinstrap beards or powdered white wigs. In the dark they could have been monsters or vampires or trolls or goblins.

And to get out, she'd have to run right past them.

Clementine took a deep breath. She steadied herself. She clenched her fists and her teeth. And she started to run.

Just as she entered their midst, one of the figures lunged at her. Clementine screamed as she ran for the exit. When she finally reached the main exit, she looked over her shoulder and saw him — the ghost!

The figure was covered in darkness, his head covered with a trooper's helmet. He limped as he walked slowly toward her and wore a gun slung over his shoulder.

Clementine ran on, her heart in her throat, but then she remembered — she had to try to communicate with the ghost. It was the only solution.

With that in mind, Clementine finally stopped running. She turned and faced the gaping entrance to the Hall of Presidents. She expected the hobbling soldier's ghost to appear at any moment. Maybe she'd see his terrified, scarred face. Or maybe he had *no* face, a mere spirit, barely connected to this worldly plane.

She stared into the darkness of the Hall of Presidents, waiting, barely breathing.

Nothing came out of the darkness. Instead, someone grabbed her shoulder from behind, and Clementine shrieked.

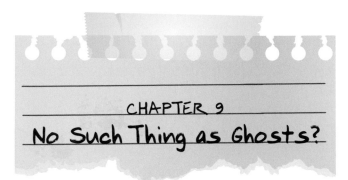

CHAPTER 9
No Such Thing as Ghosts?

"Who's there?" Wilson shouted into the darkness of the Vietnam War gallery.

"Don't try anything!" Raining shouted at the same time.

"Raining?" Wilson said.

"Wilson?" Raining said.

"Is that you?" the boys said in tandem, followed by, "I thought you were the ghost!"

Wilson felt around on the floor and found his flashlight. He switched it on and saw Raining sitting across from him in the dark doorway leading to the Vietnam War gallery.

"No such thing as ghosts, huh?" Raining said with a laugh.

"Just because they don't exist, doesn't mean I'm not afraid of them," Wilson said.

It didn't make any sense, but Raining knew just what he meant.

The two boys stood up and walked together into the gallery, following the beam of Wilson's flashlight.

"Did you find anything in the south wing?" Wilson asked.

Raining shook his head. "Nope." The south wing of the American History Museum was mostly maps and documents, as well as the three small theaters. They'd all been locked. "Did you check the north wing?"

"Nothing there either," Wilson said. He stopped in front of a diorama made up of photos of soldiers in the war. Next to it were newspaper clippings. In the middle, a video monitor was dark. When the museum was open, it showed old newsreels from the war.

Wilson studied the diorama for a few moments, then said, "I did hear footsteps."

Raining checked his friend's face, but it was as blank and disinterested as ever. "Where?" he asked.

Wilson shrugged. He kept his eyes on the diorama. "When I was in the lobby," he said. "I think it must have been you."

"Me?" Raining said.

"When I got up to check I saw someone in the central hall, and then I hurried after him," Wilson said. "Next thing I knew, I'd run into you."

"In the doorway here?" Raining said.

Wilson nodded.

"That wasn't me, then," Raining said. "I wasn't in the hallway. I was inside the gallery. After checking the document rooms, I came back here to look at the memorial photos."

"Where?" Wilson asked.

Raining pointed at the corner near the big window, next to the door Wilson had checked two days ago. "Couldn't see much," Raining added with a shrug. "Too dark."

Wilson walked toward the photo. "No footsteps in here," he said. "Carpeting."

"Told you it wasn't me," Raining said.

The boys stopped in front of the memorial photos. They studied them quietly for a few moments, hoping the images might offer a clue.

"What's so interesting about these?" Wilson asked.

Raining stepped up to the big mural, a huge color photo of the Vietnam Veterans Memorial in Washington, D.C. He pointed at a figure in the photo — an old man with a curved back and a cane, his face inches from the gleaming and dark stone wall of the memorial.

"That's my grandfather," Raining said.

Wilson leaned closer. "Really?"

Raining nodded. "My dad wanted his father in the photo, so they got it special," he said. "One of the perks of working at the museum."

"Cool," Wilson said. "I didn't know your grandpa was in the Army. Was he drafted?"

"He was in the Marines," Raining said. "He enlisted the day he turned eighteen."

Raining grew quiet as he studied the image. He would be eighteen in only six years. He could hardly imagine going through what his grandfather had endured.

Wilson coughed into his fist, bringing Raining back to the present.

"We should probably find the girls," Raining said. He turned to Wilson with a wicked grin and added in his gloomiest voice, "Unless Clementine has already been captured by the ghost and dragged into the nightmare realm to be his bride!"

Wilson laughed and led the way out into the hall, shining his flashlight beam in front of them. Ghost or no ghost, this time he wanted to see where he was going.

CHAPTER 10
Ghost Hunting

Across the museum, Clementine was having a run-in of her own.

"What are you doing around here?" a voice growled in Clementine's ear. "I heard a lot of screaming!"

Clementine turned around and came face to face with a woman a foot taller than she was. She was dressed head to toe in the stark blue uniform of a Capitol City Museum guard.

"I thought you were the ghost!" Clementine said.

The guard snarled and let go of Clementine's shoulder. "Ghost!" the guard snapped. "I don't buy into that nonsense. Now why don't you tell me why you're skulking around my museum like a thief in the night!"

"Not a thief!" Clementine protested. "A ghost hunter!"

The guard gritted her teeth and puffed up her cheeks until Clementine thought she was just about ready to explode. But she didn't explode. Instead she took Clementine by the wrist and snapped, "Come with me."

* * *

Amal, meanwhile, was halfway across the museum. She'd wandered away from the bathroom after Clementine had gone inside. She'd planned to be there when Clementine came out but had somehow missed her. When Amal had returned to the bathroom and poked her head inside, Clementine had disappeared.

Amal had walked up and down the entire length of the staff-only area and had just returned to the main part of the museum when she heard her friend's distinctive screaming.

"Uh oh," Amal said to herself, taking off in the direction of the screams. "Sounds like Clementine found her poltergeist."

But when Amal made it to the main hallway, she didn't find Clementine cowering against the wall, nor did she find the angry spirit of an American soldier airing its grievances with humanity. Instead she found a museum guard dragging her friend by the wrist through the hall toward the security office.

"What's going on here?" Amal said, trailing after them.

The guard laughed a little. It sounded like a truck coughing exhaust. "You might as well come along too," she said. "I don't care who your parents are, roaming around the museum after hours is forbidden!"

"Since when?" Amal snapped, but the guard ignored her.

When they reached the security office, the guard opened the door. "That's weird," she muttered to herself. "This should have been locked."

Clementine and Amal exchanged a glance. Either the ghost was going around the museum and picking locks, or . . .

"Raining and Wilson!" Amal exclaimed. Sure enough, there they were, sitting next to each other on the bench along the wall of the office. The other guard on-duty sat at the desk, scowling.

"I found these two skulking around the Vietnam War gallery," said the scowling guard, a young man with a neat beard and a scar under his right eye.

"And I found these two outside the Hall of Presidents," said the guard who'd escorted Amal and Clementine. "I'd say that settles the ghost question."

"What do you mean?" asked the guard at the desk.

"Isn't it obvious?" said the burly woman. "These four brats have been running wild after hours, night after night. As a matter of fact, two of these kids were the first ones to 'see' the ghost."

Amal smiled, and Raining lowered his head.

"And, I might be wrong, but I would bet you dollars to doughnuts that this girl right here" — she gave Clementine's wrist a tug — "is the one who spoke to the news people about the haunting."

"Is that right?" the guard at the desk asked, raising an eyebrow.

Clementine blushed.

"Thought so," said the other guard. She let go of Clementine's wrist — finally — and motioned toward the bench. "You two, have a seat with your friends. I'll call your parents." With that, she passed through the main part of the office, stepped through an interior door, and closed it behind her.

The younger guard looked the four friends over. "Is it true?" he said.

"Is what true?" Raining said. "We don't believe in the ghost either."

"I do," Clementine interjected. "Just saying."

The guard tapped his finger on the desk, like he was thinking about something. "Well, I'll tell you," he said. "I don't mind the haunting stuff one bit.

It's gotten lots of attention for the Vietnam War gallery, and that means attention for veterans."

"It does?" Raining said. "Why?"

"Well, for starters, the museum is donating a portion of ticket sales to a charity to help U.S. vets," the guard explained. "The donations box in the gallery itself has been stuffed solid for the past couple of days."

"Wow," Raining said. "All because of the ghost?"

The guard nodded. "Your friend here helped too," he said, nodding toward Clementine, "by getting on the news."

Clementine blushed again. Raining had been mad at her for calling so much attention to the museum, but maybe it had been a good thing.

"And secondly," the guard went on, "any time people are talking about veterans and the raw deal they often get, it's a good thing, if you ask me."

"Were you in the Vietnam War?" Amal asked.

The guard laughed. "No, I wasn't even born yet!" he said. He stood up as the door behind him opened, and the other guard stepped out.

"Dr. Sam is on his way here now," she said. "And he didn't sound happy to be interrupted."

Raining slouched on the bench in despair. "Great," he said. "So now the investigation is over, and my dad is mad at us. Again."

CHAPTER 11
Faking

The next morning, Raining and Wilson were back at the museum bright and early. There had been no ghost-sightings since the security guards had nabbed them and the girls the night before. It was July third, and the museum was extra crowded. Raining figured the people of Capitol City got extra patriotic this close to Independence Day. The ghost story probably wasn't hurting either.

"I've been thinking," Wilson said as the two boys strolled through the Vietnam War gallery, where extra security had been stationed. "If you and Amal *did* see someone here the other night, he had to have left through the emergency exit."

"But there's an alarm on it," Raining pointed out. "It would have gone off."

"Unless it's broken," Wilson said. He stopped in front of the heavy black door. A red-and-white sticker very clearly stated: *Alarm Will Sound.*

"You want to test it?" Raining said.

Wilson shook his head. They'd gotten in enough trouble the night before.

"Me either," Raining agreed. "Any other brilliant ideas?"

"Yes," Wilson said. "If there are footprints on the other side of this door, it would mean someone went through it recently."

"So?" Raining said. "Even if someone went through it, that doesn't mean it was the ghost."

"Do you think this door gets a lot of use?" Wilson said. "Has there been an emergency in the museum lately?"

"No," Raining admitted. "That's a good point. So if we find footprints, the ghost went out this way. Which means there's no ghost."

"Just someone pretending to be a ghost," Wilson agreed.

"Why would someone do that?" Raining asked.

Wilson didn't answer — mostly because he didn't *have* an answer.

"So how do we check for footprints if we can't open the door?" Raining asked.

"We need a key to deactivate the alarm," Wilson said as they walked past a pair of security guards — the same ones who'd busted them the night before — stationed nearby. The female guard was watching them closely. "Where can we get one?"

The security guard, overhearing Wilson's comment, looked at him. Then she looked over at Raining. Then she looked back at Wilson. "You have got to be kidding," she finally said.

"Look," Wilson said. "You want to catch whoever is faking this ghost stuff as much as we do, right?"

"Sure," said the guard.

"And we need that key to check for clues," Wilson went on.

"You're actually asking me," the guard said, bending down so she could glare at the boys from closer range, "to just hand

over the key to the museum's emergency exit doors?"

"Yes," Wilson said.

"No," the guard snapped. "I'm going on rounds now." With that, she stomped off, leaving the boys behind.

The second, seemingly nicer guard let out a chuckle. "She sure doesn't like you," he said.

"You think?" Raining said. "Is she always this cranky?"

The guard shrugged. "She gets like this around the Fourth of July," he said. He stepped away from the boys and walked across the gallery, limping a little.

"Why?" Raining said. "Doesn't she like independence?"

The guard chuckled. "It's the fireworks," he said. "They make her jumpy."

"My dog is like that too," Wilson said.

"Your dog probably didn't do combat duty in the Iraq War," the guard said. "Off you two go, and stay out of trouble."

"We will," Raining said. He hurried Wilson along until they were well out of earshot. "Did you hear that?"

Wilson nodded. "The grumpy guard is a veteran," he said. "We might have found our ghost."

"Let's go out to the Big Lawn," Raining suggested. "We can find that emergency exit from the outside and maybe we'll get lucky."

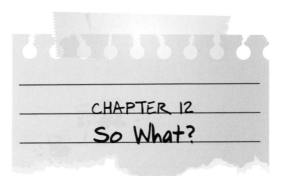

CHAPTER 12
So What?

"Then it's her!" Amal said. She grinned, bringing her fist down into her open palm. "It has to be."

The girls had hurried down to the museum after Raining had texted them about what they'd discovered about the security guard. While they'd waited, the boys had tracked down the opposite side of emergency exit they'd seen from the inside.

Sure enough, they'd found faint footprints in the dirt outside the door. Thanks to the storm earlier in the week, the ground had been wet enough to preserve them.

Now the four friends strolled across the Big Lawn where the finishing touches were being put on the Fourth of July festival. It would officially begin in the morning with the All-American Breakfast sponsored by the museums. At the end of a long day of fun, the fireworks would cap off the event.

"Why does it have to be her?" Clementine asked. "You just *want* it to be her because she's mean."

"You're one to talk," Wilson said. "Does the name Ruthie Rothchild mean anything to you? How many times have you accused her of being behind something?"

Clementine's face went beet red. Ruthie was a classmate of hers, and whenever anything went wrong — or there was any mystery to solve — Clementine had a tendency to cast blame Ruthie's way.

"I haven't even mentioned her name in ages!" Clementine protested. She looked down meekly. "I'm trying not to, you know."

"Anyway," Amal said, "here's what we know so far — the ghost has been great for the museum *and* veterans' charities."

"Plus," Wilson added, "Raining and I found footprints outside the emergency exit, so chances are that's how our 'ghost' got out of the Vietnam War gallery the other night."

"And," Raining finished, "only the security guards have keys to deactivate the alarms on the emergency exits."

Clementine sat on a bench at the edge of the festival grounds. "The thing is," she said, "so what?"

"What do you mean, so what?" Wilson said. "Are you annoyed because we proved it wasn't a ghost?"

"Well," Clementine drawled, "you haven't. You've proven that *if* it wasn't a ghost then it was *probably* the grouchy guard. But still — so what?"

"Why do you keep saying that?" Amal asked her.

Raining sat beside Clementine. "She's right," he said. "So what? The guard hasn't broken any laws. She hasn't hurt anyone. And she's *supposed* to be wandering the museum at night, right? She's a security guard."

"Oh," Wilson said, and he sat down too. "I see your point."

Amal stomped her foot. "Then we can't even turn her in!" she said. "There's no point in even telling your dad," she added to Raining.

"Nope," Clementine agreed, shaking her head.

"So now what?" Raining asked.

Clementine stood up and pulled an elastic band from her wrist. "I'm going home," she said, pulling her long hair into a ponytail. "I'll see you back here in the morning, okay?"

"Sure," Raining said. He couldn't help feeling a little down. For two days, it was all he and his friends had thought about, and now it didn't even matter.

Raining got a ride home from his dad that evening. His dad caught his eye in the rearview mirror.

"You all right?" Dad said.

Raining shrugged. "I'm fine."

"You don't seem fine," Dad said.

Raining didn't answer. He just stared out the window, watching the tree-lined streets of his neighborhood roll by. Before long, Dad pulled up in front of their house.

Before they got out, though, Raining said, "We figured out who's behind all the ghost stuff at the museum."

Dad spun in his seat and stared at his son. "You what?"

Raining nodded.

"So who is it?" Dad asked.

"The grouchy security guard," Raining said. "The woman. I don't know her name."

"You mean Patricia?" Dad said. He shook his head. "It couldn't be her."

Raining leaned forward, shocked. "What? Why not?"

Dad unbuckled his seat belt and opened his door. As he climbed out of the car, he said, "Patricia was on vacation until yesterday. She was visiting her sister in Florida. She even sent a postcard."

Raining fell back in his seat. He had to call his friends.

CHAPTER 13
Much-Needed Attention

The next day, the four sleuths barely took part in the Fourth of July festivities. They had breakfast and watched the museum productions of famous speeches and the reenactment of the battle at Lexington and Concord. But they didn't cheer, and they didn't smile, and they didn't play any of the carnival games the museums had set up.

It was hot dogs, turkey dogs, and veggie dogs for lunch. The kids took the dogs they preferred and found a spot to sit on the grass at the edge of the festival grounds. Seated in a circle, with Clementine and Amal facing the festival and Wilson and Raining facing the back of the American History Museum, they had their lunch. They didn't talk much. After what Raining had told them the night before, no one had much to say.

Raining stared at the museum. From where he sat, he could see the emergency exit — the one he and Wilson had checked. He could see the big window in the Vietnam War gallery. He could even see the two soldiers — the mannequins — with their helmets on and guns slung over their shoulders.

As Raining watched, a third soldier moved slowly into view. He wore the same helmet, and leaned something long and narrow against his shoulder.

"Raining," Wilson said quietly beside him, staring intently at the big window, "isn't the museum closed today?"

"Yup," Raining said.

"Then who's that?" Wilson had spotted the third soldier too.

The girls twisted around to see.

"See?" Clementine said. "It *is* a ghost."

Raining shook his head. "It can't be," he said.

Amal took an angry bite of her turkey dog. "No way," she agreed with her mouth full.

Clementine, though, flashed a smile and took a big bite of her veggie dog. She looked truly happy.

"Let's focus on a new mystery," Wilson said, turning away. "What are we going to do this afternoon?"

Clementine and Amal both turned away too and started chatting with Wilson about the plan for the rest of the day. In moments, the three friends were deep in conversation.

Raining, however, kept watching the window, and a moment later the emergency exit opened. No alarm went off. But Raining saw him. The young security guard walked down the big iron staircase leading from the emergency exit. He wore no helmet, but as he held the railing and descended, he carried his cane against his shoulder.

The young guard strode past their picnic spot. Raining hopped up and followed him.

"I'll be right back," he called back to his friends, hurrying to catch up with the guard.

When he was just behind him, Raining said quietly, "Why'd you do it?"

The guard stopped and smiled. "Figured me out, huh?"

"Barely," Raining said. "I saw you just now. We thought it was Patricia."

"Pat?" the guard said. He shook his head. "She'd never. And if she knew I did this . . . ooh boy."

"She wouldn't like it?" Raining said. "But she's a vet."

The guard nodded. "That's why I did it," he said. "I see how hard she works and how tough she has it. But it's not her style to call attention to herself — or to her military record. But someone should. Someone should make sure people know how much veterans have done for this country."

"But how did you know anyone would even see you?" Raining asked.

"I know you kids are always hanging around the museum after hours," the guard replied. "I've seen you there myself. I figured if I could get you and your friends to see me — and think I was a ghost — you'd be sure to make some noise about it. An adult might not have fallen for it, but a bunch of kids? Who better to start rumors about ghosts? That's all I really needed to bring attention to the exhibit and veterans' sacrifices."

"You're a good friend," Raining said.

The guard patted Raining's shoulder. "You are too," he said. He thumbed over his shoulder. "And yours seem to be waiting for you."

Raining stopped, letting the guard walk on into the festival without him, and turned around. He watched Clementine smile as she ate. He could just hear Amal ranting on about something — she seemed happiest when she ranted, somehow. He could practically feel Wilson's brain working, struggling with the mystery of the ghost, even though he'd said it didn't matter. Maybe he'd figure it out or maybe not.

But Raining decided then and there not to tell them — or anyone.

Steve B.

About the Author

Steve Brezenoff is the author of more than fifty middle-grade chapter books, including the Field Trip Mysteries series, the Ravens Pass series of thrillers, and the Return to Titanic series. In his spare time, he enjoys video games, cycling, and cooking. Steve lives in Minneapolis with his wife, Beth, and their son and daughter.

Lisa W.

About the Illustrator

Lisa K. Weber is an illustrator currently living in Oakland, California. She graduated from Parsons School of Design in 2000 and then began freelancing. Since then, she has completed many print, animation, and design projects, including graphic novelizations of classic literature, character and background designs for children's cartoons, and textiles for dog clothing.

GLOSSARY

contemplation (kon-tuhm-PLEY-shuhn) — the act of thinking deeply about something

dejected (dih-JEK-tid) — sad because of loss or failure

diorama (dahy-uh-RAM-uh) — a life-size exhibit with realistic natural surroundings and a painted background

exhibit (eg-ZIB-it) — a public display of works of art, historical objects, etc.

gallery (GAL-uh-ree) — a room or building in which people look at paintings, sculptures, etc.

impostor (im-POS-ter) — a person who deceives others by pretending to be someone else

melancholy (MEL-uhn-kol-ee) — a sad mood or feeling

naïve (nah-EEV) — having a lack of experience or knowledge

silhouette (sil-oo-ET) — a dark shape in front of a light background; the shape or outline of something

tremendous (trih-MEN-duhs) — very large or great

DISCUSSION QUESTIONS

1. Do you think the younger security guard was right to do what he did? Were his actions justified? Talk about why you agree or disagree with his actions.

2. Put yourself in Raining's shoes. Do you think what he did at the end of this story was the right decision? Talk about whether or not you would have shared the truth about the soldier's ghost with your friends.

3. One of the major issues in this case was whether or not ghosts even exist. Do you think ghosts exist? Talk about which side of the argument you fall on. Be prepared to defend your position!

WRITING PROMPTS

1. At the end of this story, Raining tells the younger security guard he is a good friend. Do you agree with that? Write a paragraph about what it means to be a good friend.

2. Clementine and her friends don't seem to agree on the existence of ghosts. Write a few paragraphs about a time you and a friend had a difference of opinions. How did you resolve it?

3. Imagine you were tasked with solving the mystery of the soldier's ghost. Write a paragraph about how you would have done so and who else you might have considered as a suspect.

MORE ABOUT THE VIETNAM WAR

The Vietnam War officially lasted for more than twenty years, from 1954 to 1975, making it the longest war in which the United States has ever participated. It is also one of the most unpopular wars the United States has even been involved in.

Prior to the start of the Vietnam War, Vietnam was divided into North Vietnam and South Vietnam. At the root of the conflict was the North Vietnamese government's desire to unify the country under a single communist regime, similar to those in China and the Soviet Union. The South Vietnamese government, on the other hand, fought to preserve a Vietnam more closely tied to the West. The conflict pitted the communist government of North Vietnam and its allies in South Vietnam, known as the Viet Cong, against the government of South Vietnam and its main ally, the United States.

The first U.S. troops entered Vietnam in March 1965, and for four years, the majority of the fighting took place between North Vietnamese and U.S. forces. By 1969, more than five hundred thousand U.S. troops were stationed in Vietnam. However by 1973, the costs and casualties of the war proved to be too great, and the United States withdrew its troops. Two years later, Vietnam was unified under communist control.

Overall, more than three million people, including nearly two million Vietnamese civilians, were killed over the course of the conflict. In 1982, the Vietnam Veterans Memorial, which was designed by 21-year-old Yale University student Maya Lin, was unveiled in Washington, D.C. The memorial was inscribed with the names of the 57,939 U.S. troops who had died or were missing as a result of the war. Over the years, additions to the memorial have brought that total to more than 58,000 names. The Vietnam Veterans Memorial remains one of the most-visited memorials in Washington, D.C., attracting millions of visitors each year.

1091